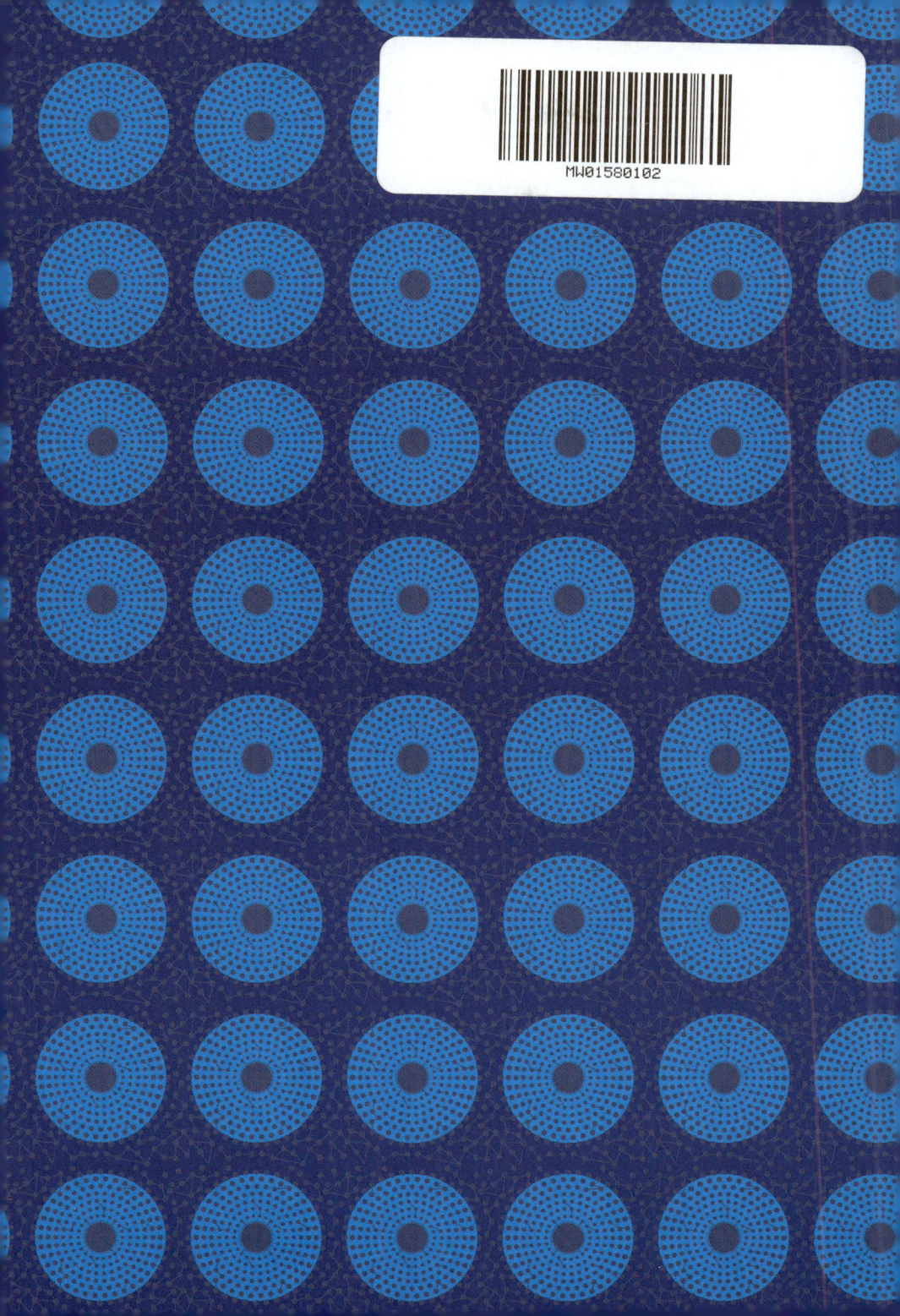

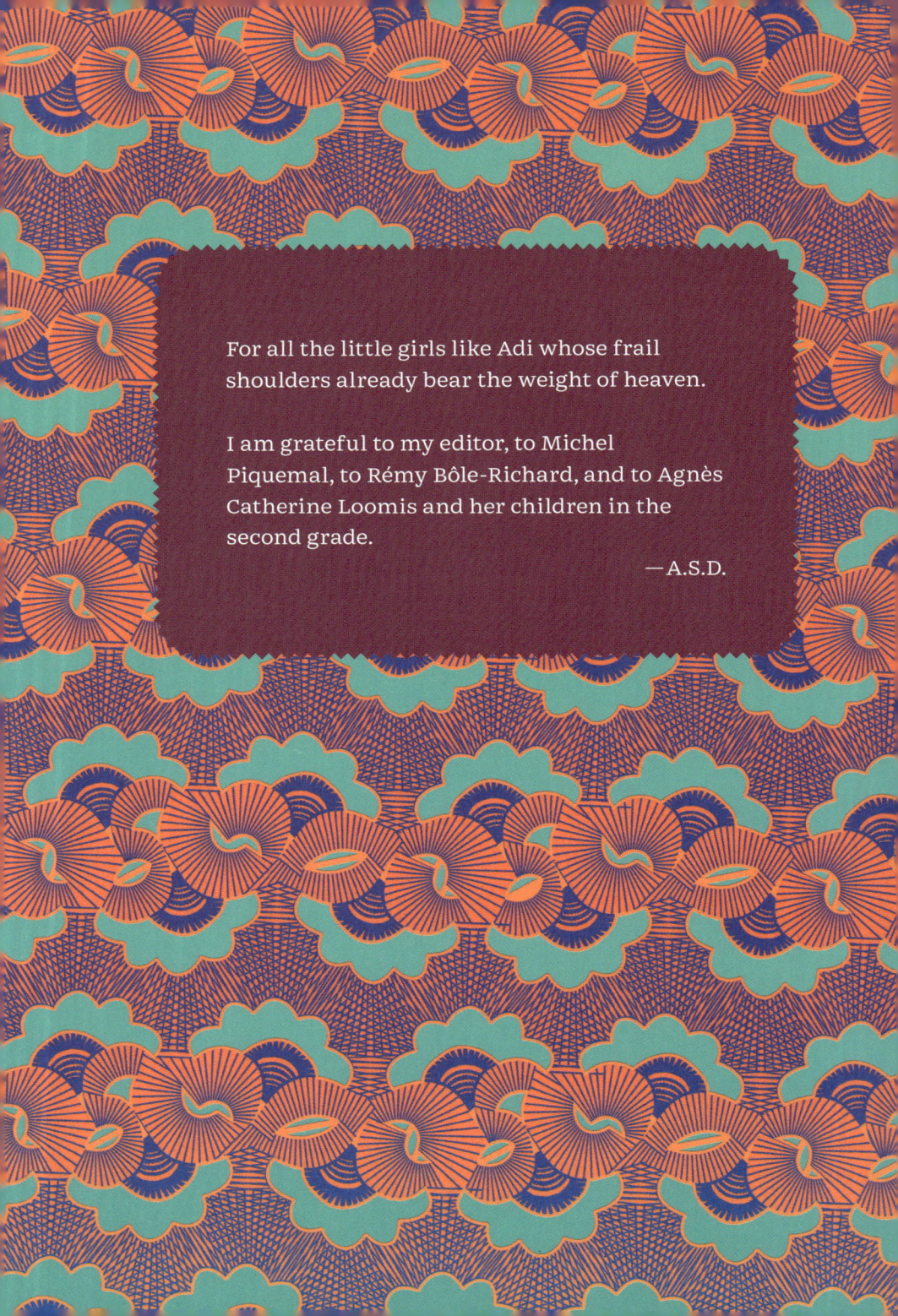

For all the little girls like Adi whose frail shoulders already bear the weight of heaven.

I am grateful to my editor, to Michel Piquemal, to Rémy Bôle-Richard, and to Agnès Catherine Loomis and her children in the second grade.

—A.S.D.

Adi of BouTanga

A STORY FROM CAMEROON

Alain Serge Dzotap   *Marc Daniau*

Translation by the author

EERDMANS BOOKS FOR YOUNG READERS
GRAND RAPIDS, MICHIGAN

My name is Adi.

Adi is short for Adidjatou. I haven't always lived in Boutanga, on the slopes of the high green hill. I come from Maka 2, not far from Maka 1, our twin village. Our village lies on the banks of the great river, a little lost among the tall grasses. I call them "chameleon grasses": they change color with the seasons, like chameleons stealing the color of everything they touch.

    Our village isn't really ours. We Mbororos are nomadic herders, always on the lookout for abundant

grass and water for our herds. "This way, there's no risk of our feet taking root," Dad often jokes. My teacher at school says something similar: "Rooting is like when the fence post of the living hedge develops roots, because

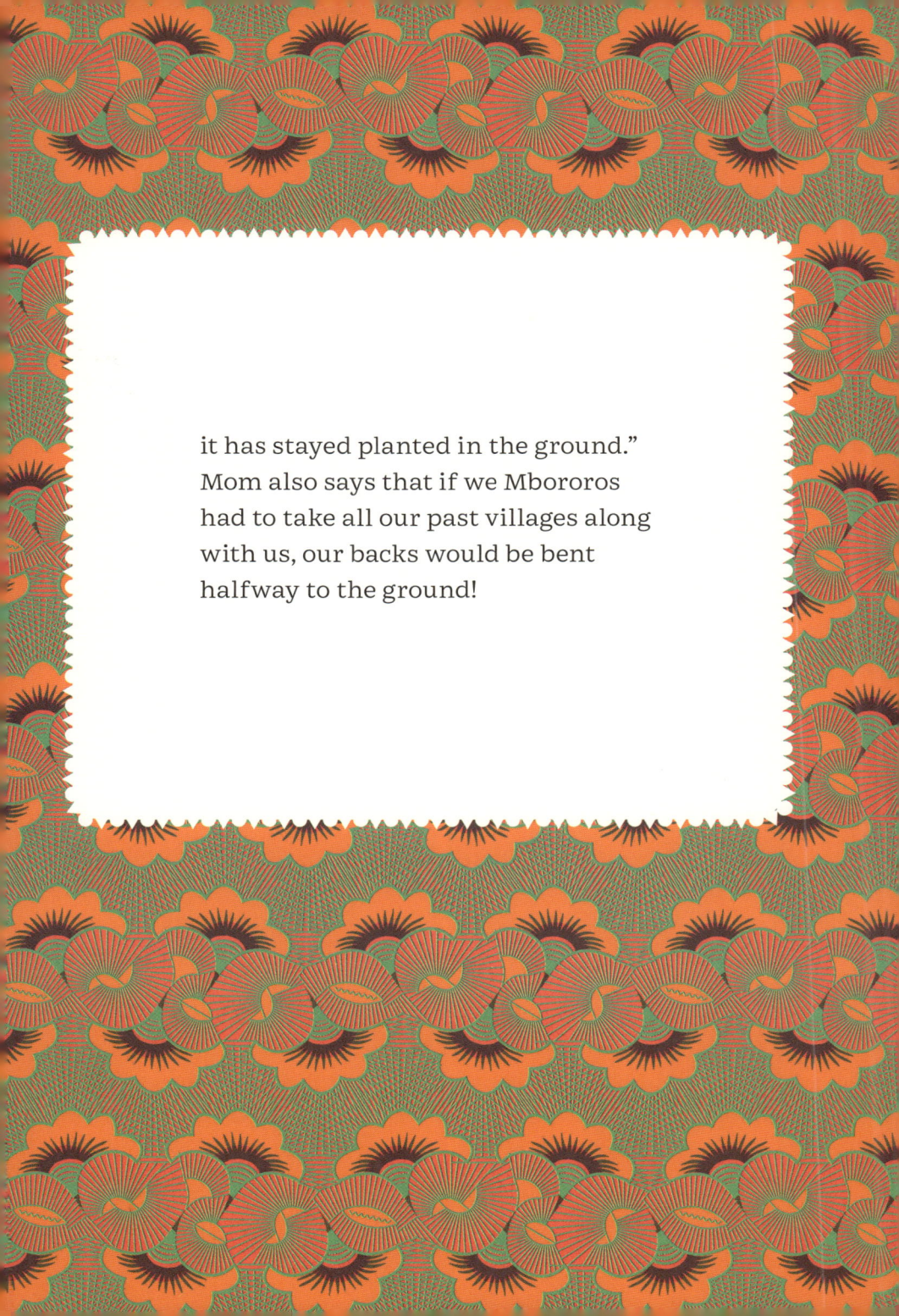

it has stayed planted in the ground."
Mom also says that if we Mbororos
had to take all our past villages along
with us, our backs would be bent
halfway to the ground!

I was born in the village on the banks of the great river, the village of the great chameleon grasses. I'm now thirteen dry seasons and as many rainy seasons old. And I know that no one wants to leave, to abandon the village of the great chameleon grasses. But no matter how hard I look at my feet and those of people passing by, I can't see any roots growing. This habit sometimes intrigues Zouliatou, who laughs at me:

"Looking for a needle, Adidjatou?" she asks.

Every time, I joke: "No, I dropped my nose!"

And Zouliatou laughs even harder. I imitate her.

In fact, like those tall grasses that change color, almost everyone in our village has changed jobs. Dad, for example, is no longer a security guard for the company building the roads in our village.

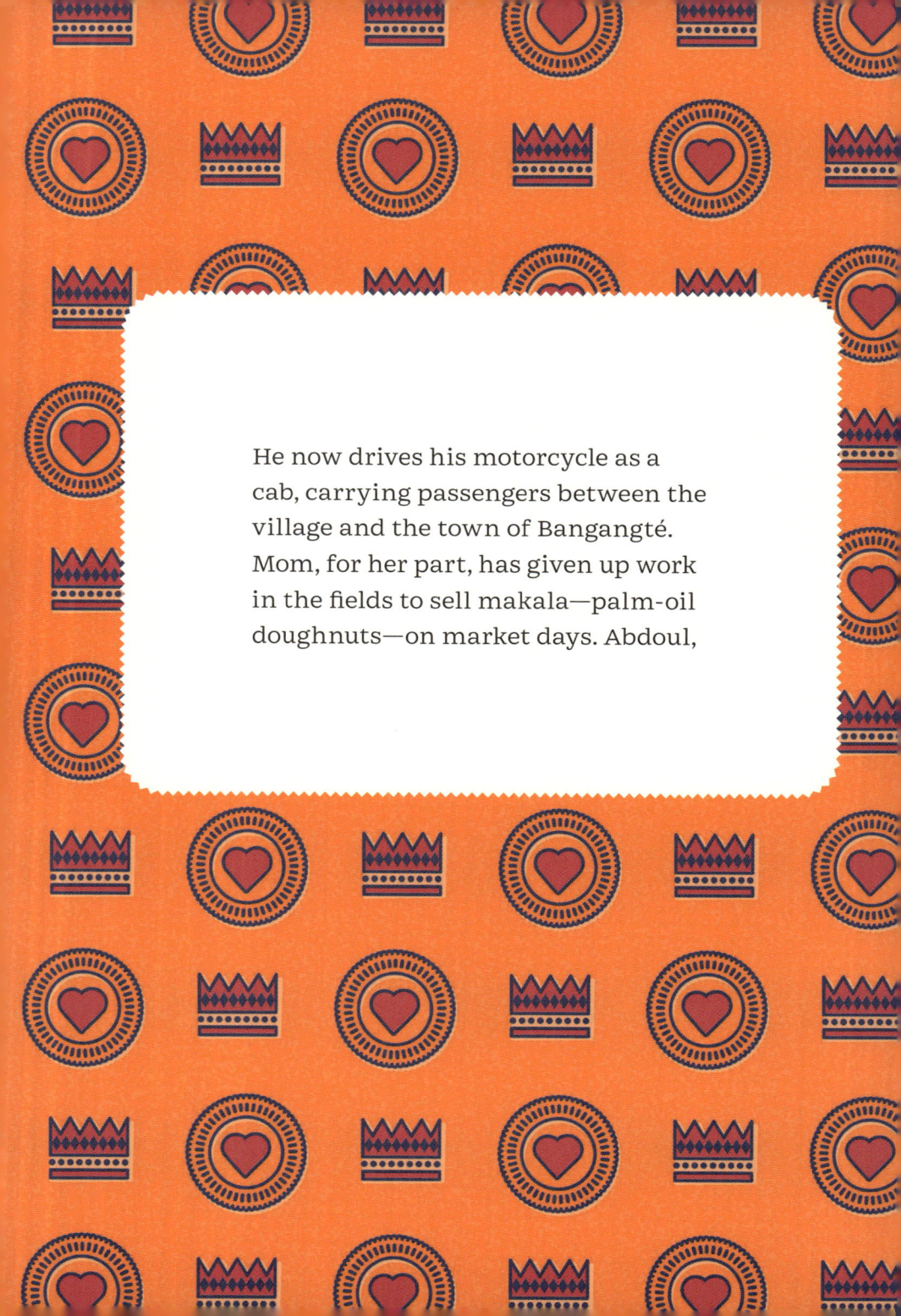

He now drives his motorcycle as a cab, carrying passengers between the village and the town of Bangangté. Mom, for her part, has given up work in the fields to sell makala—palm-oil doughnuts—on market days. Abdoul, whose herd of oxen was decimated by a strange disease, has become a shoemaker. But I prefer to stay the big sister of Fadimatou, Zénabou, Youssoufa, Daïrou, Souaïbou, and baby Mohamadou.

I go to the only school in the village. Our school was a gift. Mama Ly and Monsieur gave it to our village so that all the children could come and learn to read and write. Mama Ly is very kind. Sometimes, when she visits our classroom, she takes us in her arms. Her perfume seems to be a mixture of a thousand wildflowers.

Before the school was given to our village, words were invisible to us. We could hear them, but we couldn't see or touch them. I even thought a strong wind might steal them as soon as they left our mouths.

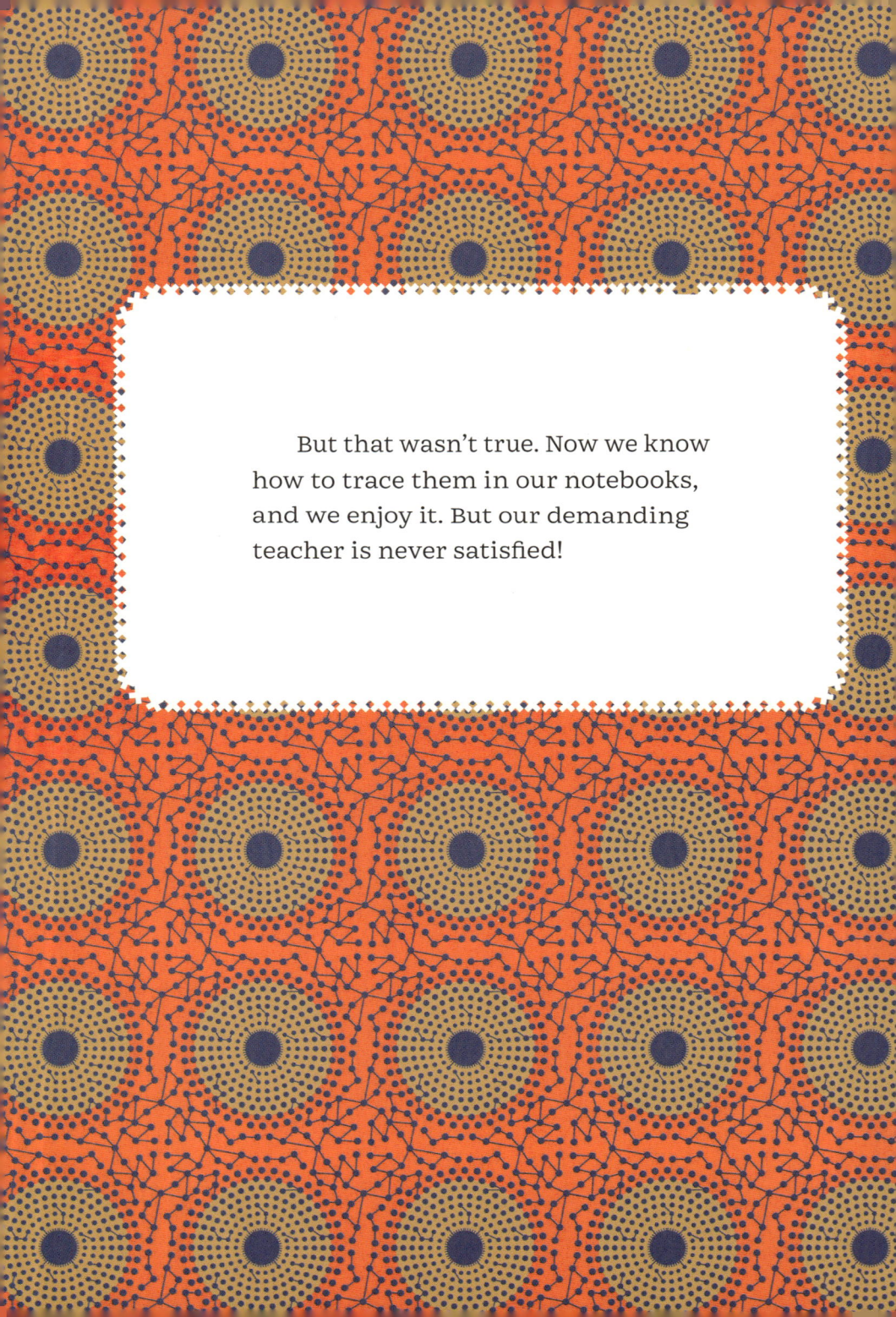

But that wasn't true. Now we know how to trace them in our notebooks, and we enjoy it. But our demanding teacher is never satisfied!

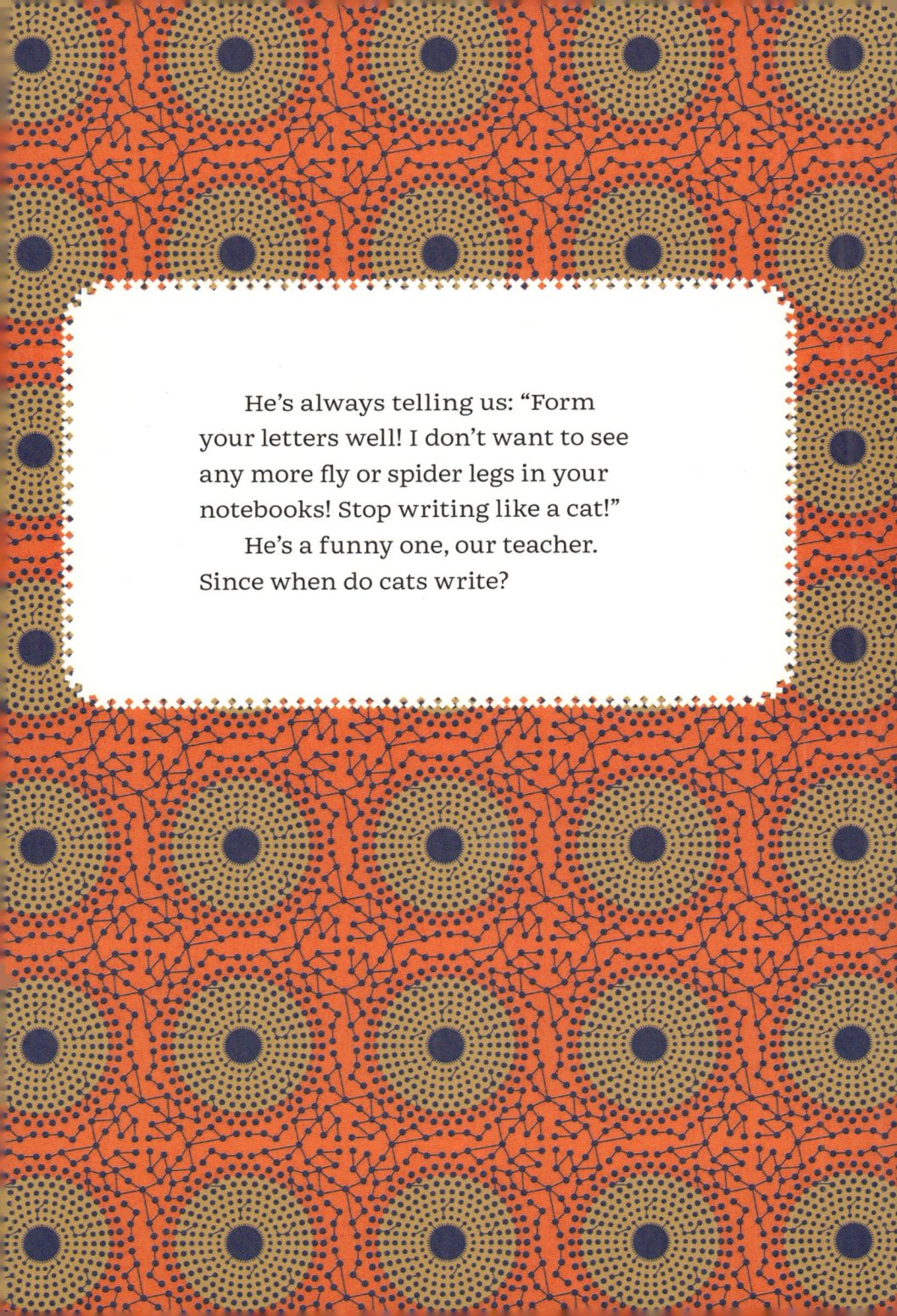

He's always telling us: "Form your letters well! I don't want to see any more fly or spider legs in your notebooks! Stop writing like a cat!"

He's a funny one, our teacher. Since when do cats write?

I am in fourth grade, and I love my school life. But I also like to make grass dolls for my little sisters, swim in the river, dance like the reeds in a storm, and try to run faster than the wind.

Sometimes I burst out laughing. And I laugh so hard that Mom teases me: "Have you swallowed a thousand weaverbirds, Adidjatou?" Mama Awa is so funny!

I exclaim: "Has anyone ever swallowed a thousand birds?"

Mom always replies: "Has anyone ever seen a little girl laugh like that?"

Then, one day, my hands start shaking too much to make grass dolls. I no longer want to dance like a reed or swim or run. I feel like an emptied burlap sack. Something has left me, probably the birds Mama Awa talked about. Because I can't laugh anymore.

Uncle Amadou has decided that I've already become a woman—even though I'm still a little girl! He has come to tell us that I must get married, like Salamatou before me, and like Mariama and so many other little girls in our village before Salamatou.

"Look, they're happy now," Uncle Amadou says, trying to win me over.

It's not true at all. Salamatou and Mariama look like young corn shoots scorched by the sun.

Under her hijab, Mom cries quietly; I do too. Dad protests. But not too loudly, so as not to upset Uncle Amadou, his big brother. Among us Mbororos, you mustn't oppose the decisions of the eldest member of the family.

Uncle Amadou leaves, but promises to come back. Dad hugs me to his chest and whispers in the hollow of my ear: "Don't worry—I won't let him."

These words dry my tears. I'm not alone; my dad is with me.

The following week, Dad makes several trips to Boutanga. I can see he's worried. He doesn't even think of taking passengers along to earn enough money to buy petrol.

More often than not, Dad isn't at home. On those days when he's away, I can sense Uncle Amadou lurking nearby. I don't dare leave the house. And on those days, I dream I'm an antelope, sinking into the red waters of the river and disappearing into the belly of a crocodile.

Another week later, Uncle Amadou comes back to see Dad.

They throw words at each other. Words that hit like stones.

"Give back the dowry you accepted for Adidjatou, because I won't trade my little girl for cows!" yells Dad.

"That's the way we've always done it in our tribe, and you're not going to change a thing!" shouts Uncle Amadou.

One morning, Dad says: "Adidjatou, pack your things. I'm going to take you to Mama Ly's. You're going to live there from now on."

I don't understand what's happening. Sure, Mama Ly is a good person, and she smells nice. But that's no reason to leave my family. Who will make grass dolls for Fadimatou? Who will braid Zénabou's hair? Who will defend Youssoufa, Daïrou, and Souaïbou when a stray ox threatens them? Who will sing lullabies to lull baby Mohamadou to sleep?

Mom explains: "This is the only solution we've found that will let you escape from your uncle and keep going to school. And this way, we can come visit you often, and I will bring you my delicious makala doughnuts."

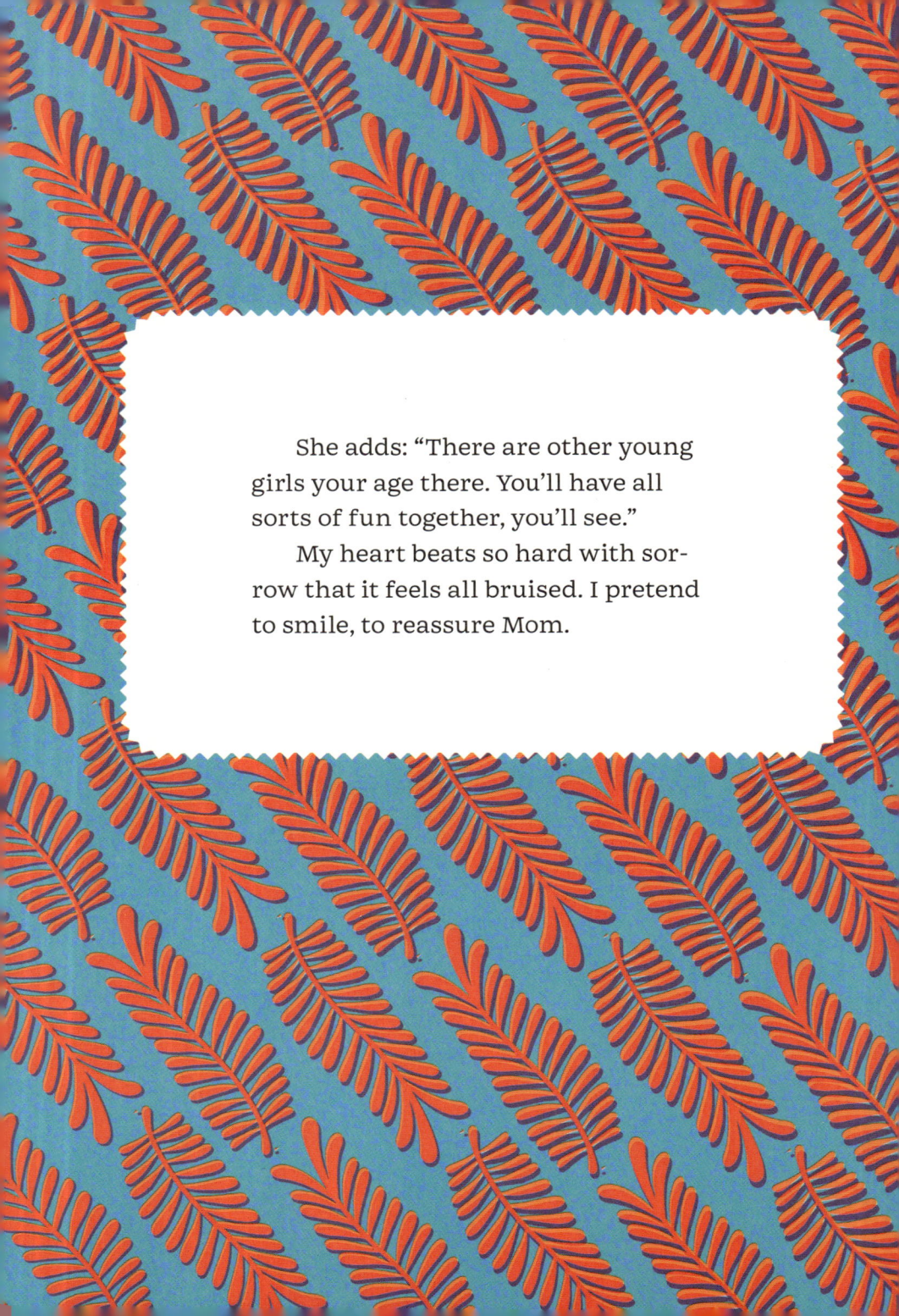

She adds: "There are other young girls your age there. You'll have all sorts of fun together, you'll see."

My heart beats so hard with sorrow that it feels all bruised. I pretend to smile, to reassure Mom.

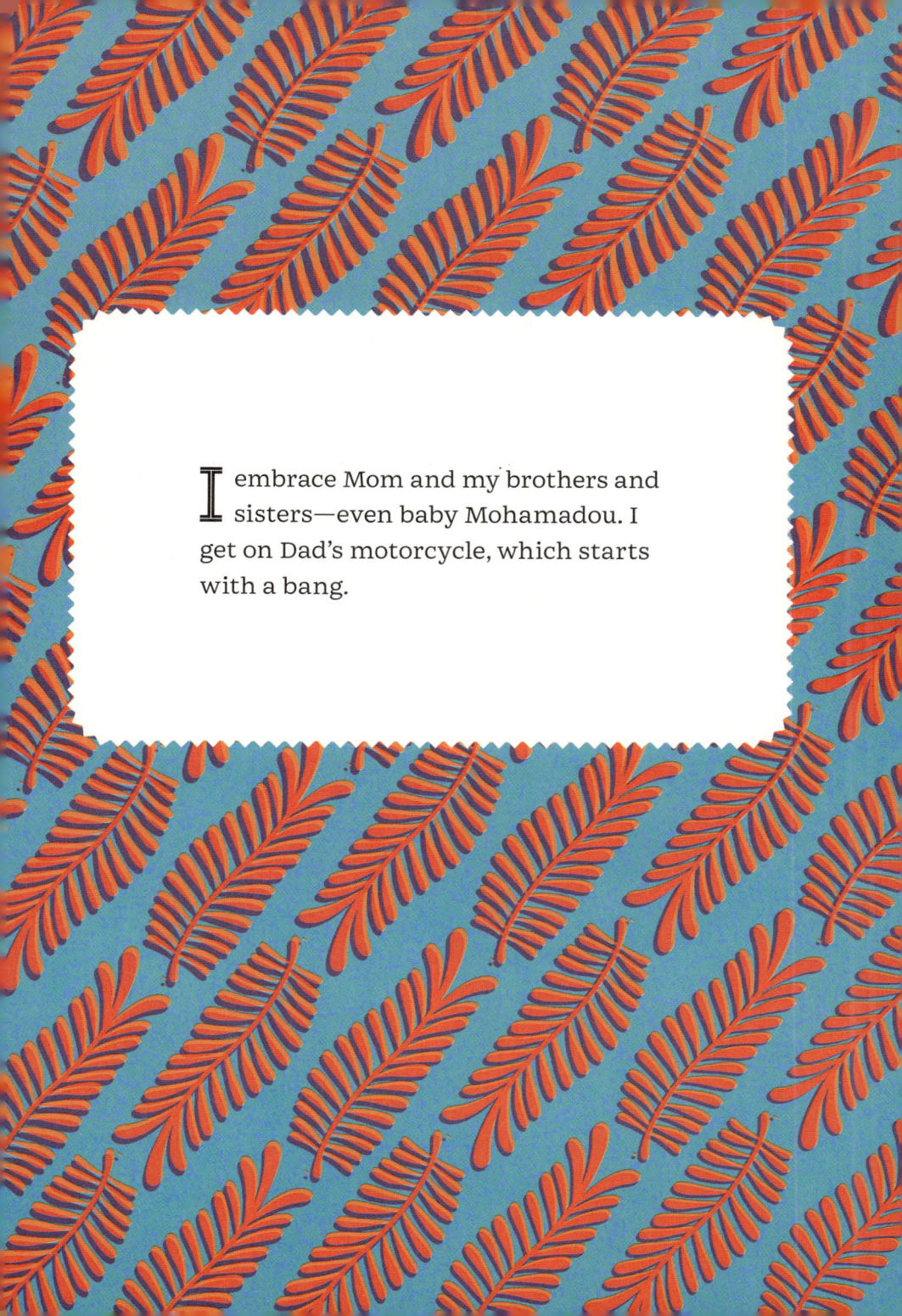

I embrace Mom and my brothers and sisters—even baby Mohamadou. I get on Dad's motorcycle, which starts with a bang.

On the road, our motorcycle and the cars create thick clouds of dust. At times, Dad slows down, because the scarlet fog prevents him from seeing into the distance. When we finally reach Boutanga, Dad's moustache is red, and my hijab is all dusty. I shake it vigorously, and it makes a last little red cloud.

    Mama Ly isn't there. Dad entrusts me to another woman. Her name is Auntie Igénie. She introduces me to the other girls.

    "Sanouh! My name is Rouga," says a young girl dressed all in blue. She must be eleven, maybe twelve.

    "Sanouh! My name is Adidjatou," I reply.

Dad's gone. I'm going to stay with Auntie Igénie for a few days. Auntie Igénie has the fingers of a fairy. She embroiders various objects with glass beads, from bracelets and necklaces to chairs, fabrics, and shoes. On her worktable, there are also little birds, elephants, and multicolored crocodiles.

"What's your name?" she asks, smiling.

"My name is Adidjatou."

"*Adi* is shorter," decides Auntie Igénie.

It's as if my name weighed as much to her as a big basket of stones. *Adidjatou*, however, feels as light to me as a hen's feather in the cool wind caressing my face.

Adi is for *Adidjatou*, just as *Rouga* is for *Roukaïyatou*. I suspect Auntie Igénie is also behind that other strange disappearance of syllables. What does she do with all those letters she removes from names? Nobody knows.

Some time later, Mama Ly comes to talk to me, with her voice as gentle as the lapping of my river. I recognize the scent of ndindim fruit and kapok tree flowers in her perfume. I still have another nine hundred and ninety-eight flowers to identify.

Mama Ly reassures me: "This is your home now. You're safe from your Uncle Amadou, and you'll never have to be afraid of him again."

Her words banish my fears. Of course, I won't be able to go back to the gift school, but I can start my school life again in this new place, far from my village of tall chameleon grass. I can play without running the risk of Uncle Amadou turning me into a sunburnt corn shoot. I'll never be like Salamatou and Mariama.

Rouga, the other girls, and I invent new games every day after school, and it's fun! Mom and Dad often bring me news from my village on the banks of the great river, and from my family. Fadimatou is now

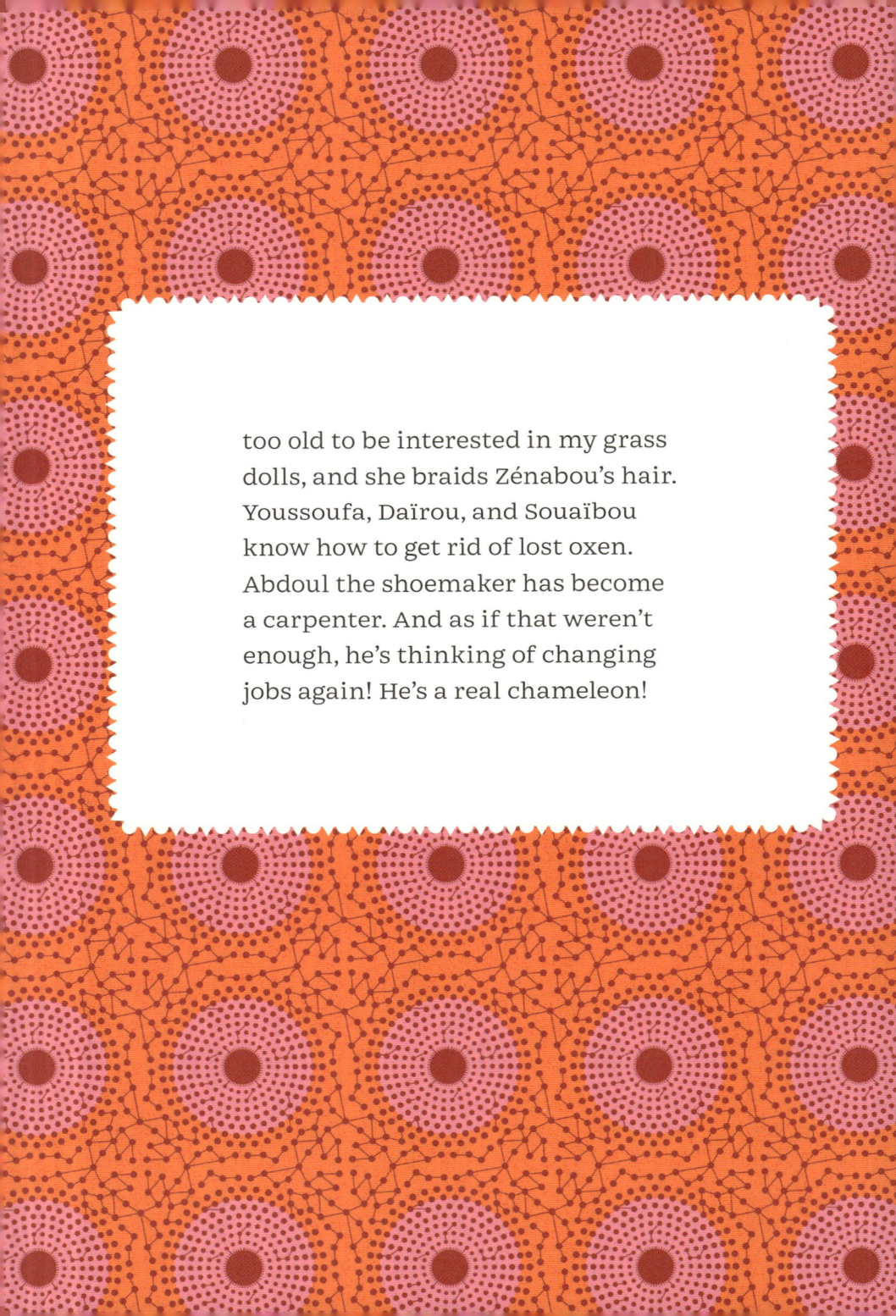

too old to be interested in my grass dolls, and she braids Zénabou's hair. Youssoufa, Daïrou, and Souaïbou know how to get rid of lost oxen. Abdoul the shoemaker has become a carpenter. And as if that weren't enough, he's thinking of changing jobs again! He's a real chameleon!

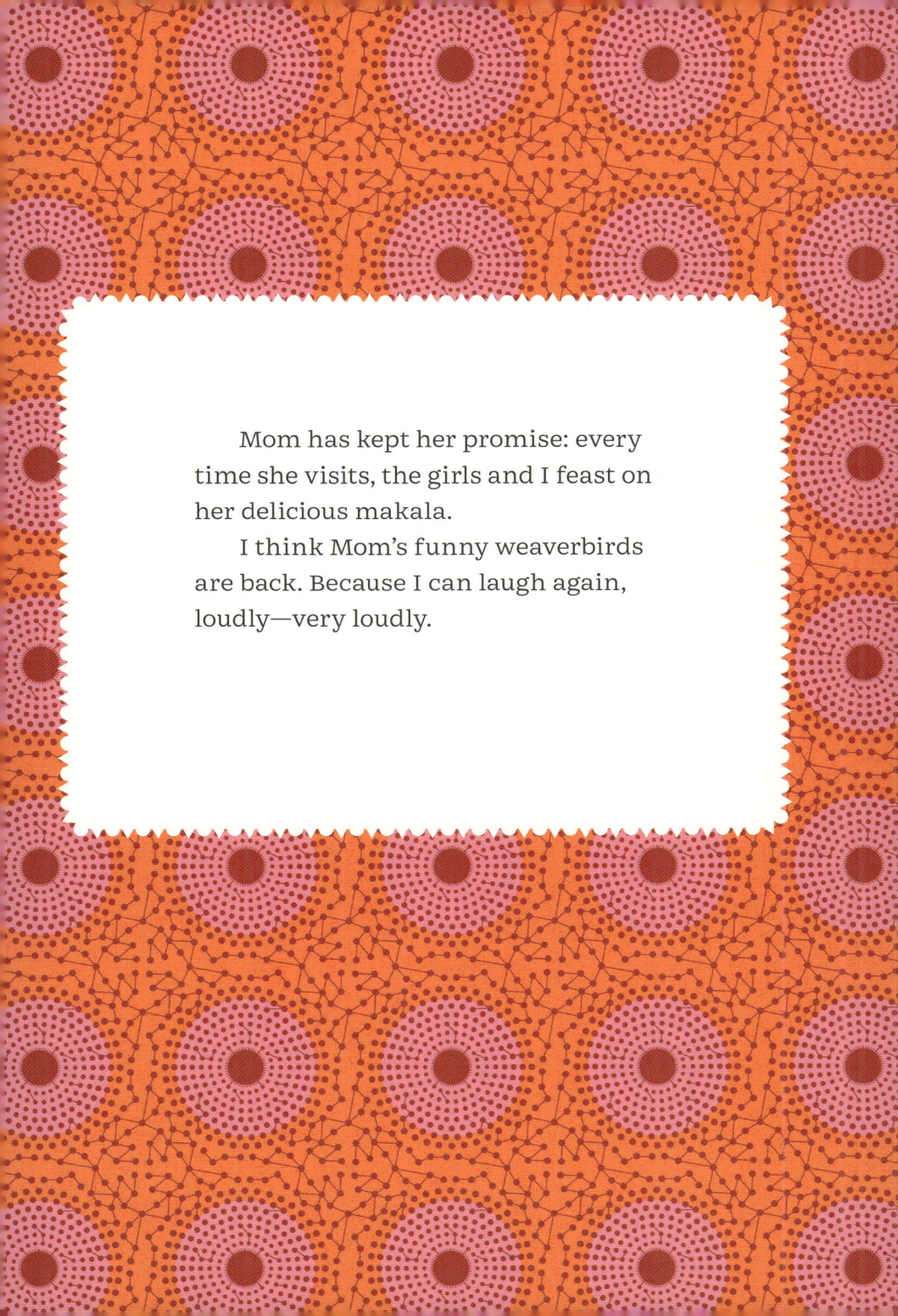

Mom has kept her promise: every time she visits, the girls and I feast on her delicious makala.

I think Mom's funny weaverbirds are back. Because I can laugh again, loudly—very loudly.

Words are curious little things. They don't just chase away our fears or dry our tears: they also express our feelings, which have grown like the fence posts in the living hedge of my chameleon-grass village.

For us, Mama Ly has become Mother. And Monsieur is no longer Monsieur, but Father. They watch over us with their big, protective arms. Mother is called Mabatngoup on special occasions. But every day, I call her Mama Sun. Because she lit the most beautiful sun above my head, just for me! But Mama Sun doesn't know that. It's just a name that stays in my heart, like a secret. In fact, it is a secret.

Today, I am twenty-two dry seasons old. When the first drops fall from the black clouds gathering in the sky, I'll also be twenty-two rainy seasons old. I'm in love with Idrissa. He often tells me that I'm the most beautiful flower in the savanna. And that's no secret . . .

   Idrissa has asked for my hand. Mama Sun, Father, Mama, and Dad all want to know what I think.
   I, Adi, say YES!
   Because Idrissa knows how to speak to my heart with his shea butter-scented words.

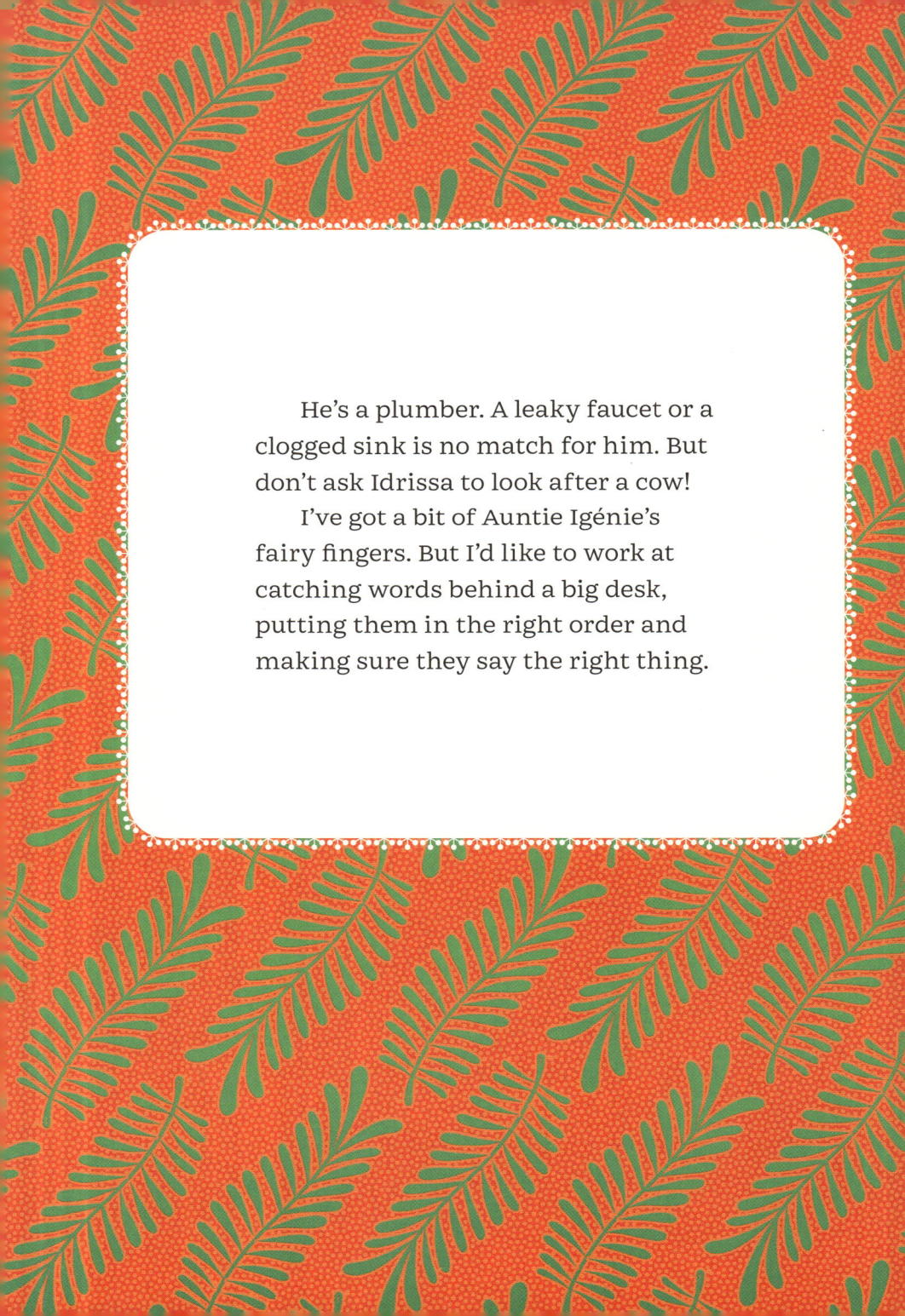

He's a plumber. A leaky faucet or a clogged sink is no match for him. But don't ask Idrissa to look after a cow!

I've got a bit of Auntie Igénie's fairy fingers. But I'd like to work at catching words behind a big desk, putting them in the right order and making sure they say the right thing.

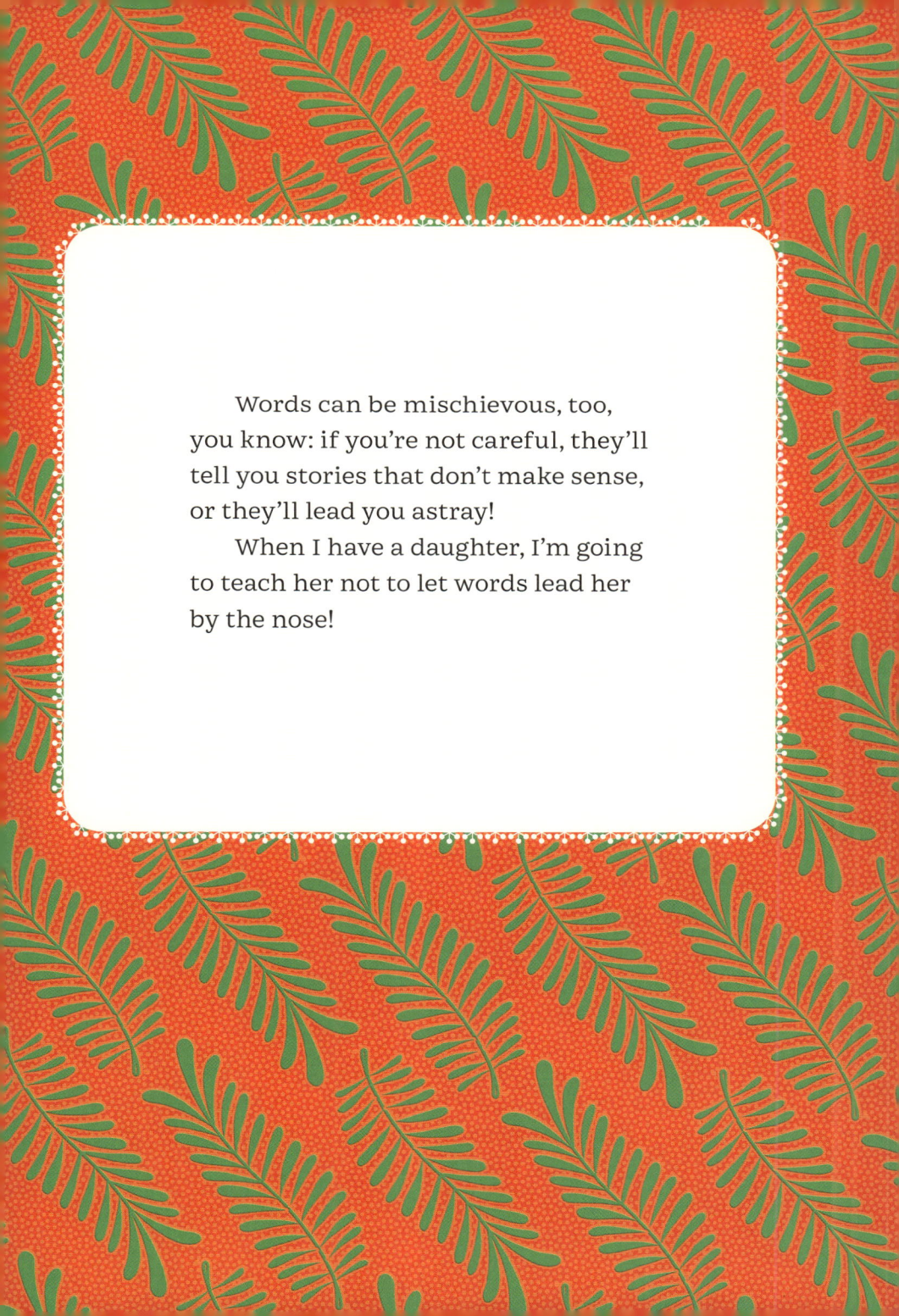

Words can be mischievous, too, you know: if you're not careful, they'll tell you stories that don't make sense, or they'll lead you astray!

When I have a daughter, I'm going to teach her not to let words lead her by the nose!

A Note from the Author

I was born in Bafoussam, Cameroon, in September 1978. There were no books in our house and no libraries in our town. My parents could neither speak nor write French or English, the two official languages of Cameroon.

As a child, I shivered with fear and laughed with joy as I listened to stories told in my mother tongue, Ndanda-Batoufam. In the same house, I heard my elders read their schoolbooks, without being able to do so myself.

I learned to read when I started elementary school, when I was about six. I knew then that books were full of stories. Stories that were happy, sad, scary, tender, or funny. Coming from a poor family, my encounter with books gave me access to thousands of lives through all the extraordinary characters I met within them. Reading opened many little windows on the world. And writing, which has become my profession, has given me the world.

From this point of view, I'm a bit like my heroine, Adi, for whom knowing how to read has been an enchantment and a blessing.

I met the real Adi in Bangoulap, when Mama Ly introduced me to this shy young girl. I immediately wanted to write her very difficult story so the world could read it. I wanted her pain and her voice to be heard, because she had dared to say no to the established social practice of forced and early marriage, which is so unjust.

I told Adi's story so that it wouldn't happen again. I meant it, and I mean it. But fighting this reality must be a daily struggle. Knowing how to read and write gave Adi the strength to push aside the walls of the world and find her place. I believe that schooling is the ideal weapon for creating a society that is a little fairer for young girls.

—Alain Serge Dzotap

*This story takes place
in Cameroon, in the highlands
where the Bamilékés live. Adi is
a real person—and her story happened
just as I've told it.*

Where is Cameroon?

The Republic of Cameroon is a country that lies between western and central Africa, with coastline along the Gulf of Guinea and borders with Nigeria, Chad, the Central African Republic, Equatorial Guinea, Gabon, and the Republic of the Congo. Cameroon is renowned for its incredible variety of cultures, languages, wildlife, and geological landscapes.

Who are the Mbororos?

The Mbororos, or Fulanis, are a nomadic people living in several African countries: Nigeria, Niger, Central African Republic, Chad, and Cameroon. Their communal activities include cattle-raising and selling goods at markets and other public places. In Cameroon, the Mbororos are settling in villages and increasingly staying in one location rather than constantly moving from one place to the next.

Who are the Bamilékés?

The people who live in Bangangté are primarily Bamilékés. They are probably descendants of the Baladis, who left medieval Egypt in the ninth century CE. After a long migration, they settled in the highlands of Cameroon's West Region. The Bamilékés are organized into around a hundred independent chiefdoms. Each is placed under the authority of a king, also known as a fô, fon, or mfen, in liaison with the Ministry of Territorial Administration. For centuries, the Bamilékés have practiced and mastered the arts of beading, woodcarving, and fabric-making. Their famous ndop cloth is sewn from indigo-dyed strips of cotton. The patterns on this fabric, reserved for the nobility, are a visual language of power and social status.

Bamilékés' architecture is considered some of the most ingenious in Sub-Saharan Africa. The square-based huts are built from a variety of local materials, including raffia bamboo, liana vine, and large, carved wooden pillars. These huts are topped with a cone-shaped thatched roof. The most imposing, called chengbundyeh, can be 30 meters (98 feet) high and 20 meters (66 feet) wide.

Who are Mama Ly and her husband?

They are a French-Cameroonian couple. A fashion designer, Mama Ly is a mabatngoup in the Bangoulap chiefdom and a member of the Bangangté royal family. "Mabatngoup" is the noble title for the greatest queens. During the prestigious elephant dance, only the mabatngoups, the king, and a few authorized notables may don the panther skin, the supreme sign of power. Her husband is a French photographer and philanthropist.

In 2002, they set up the Jean-Félicien Gacha Foundation (fondationgacha.org) in Bangoulap in tribute to Mama Ly's father. The foundation has financed, built, and equipped several nursery schools, run preventive health campaigns and birth certificate campaigns, and trained hundreds of young people in building and hotel trades. Thanks to their initiative, many young girls like Adi have benefited from quality education and training.

What is school like in Cameroon?

In Cameroon, public elementary school is free and compulsory from age six to twelve, for both boys and girls. There are also many private schools.

Unfortunately, despite all these efforts to get young people into school, in some communities, such as Adi's, girls barely out of childhood are taken out of school in order to be married off against their will.

At school, there are sometimes as many as 130 students per class, packed in like sardines. In some very poor localities, the class is held under a tree! So it is not always easy for teachers to get children to understand the lessons in mathematics, French, ICT (information and communication technology), English, history, geography, or science.

Students do typically get two breaks to play on their dusty playgrounds. They also take advantage of this time to buy sorrel juice, doughnuts, and peanut toffees from the many vendors set up in and around the school. It is a good thing they have two school breaks and the school vacations to take a breather! But in Cameroon, many students don't spend all their time relaxing, because summer vacations are also an opportunity to work in the fields and help run small family businesses, with the children selling a variety of goods: peanuts, sweets, cookies, toothpicks, mirrors, combs, scissors, carrots, and so on.

How many languages are spoken in Cameroon?

Cameroon has two official languages: French and English.

Alongside these two official languages, there are over 250 local languages and a form of slang called Camfranglais! Camfranglais is an original blend of French, English, and local languages. Want to give it a try?

Je wakayais moi ma chose tranquillement pour go au school.
 . . . means :
"I was walking without hurrying to go to school."

L'épreuve de maths est trong, je vois blanc grave!
 . . . means:
"The math test is difficult, I can't understand anything!"

If you're very beautiful, very elegant, then we'll say, *Tu es nyanga mal seulement!*

To say "I run" or "I will run" with a sense of determination, we can say *Je cours que sauf* or *Je vais sauf que courir!*

Now that you know plenty about Cameroon, we can say goodbye Cameroonian-style:

On est ensemble!—"We're together!"

Glossary

Chameleon grasses: This is a general name for the grasses in this area, rather than a particular species. In the rainy season, the grass is green. In the dry season, the grass turns yellow or gray, changing color . . . like chameleons.

Chengbundyeh: The chengbundyeh hut represents the unity of the people, as it is built with the participation of everyone. It houses the council of nine wise men, descendants of the kingdom's founders. They meet in the chengbundyeh to make the most important decisions.

Dowry: This is the sum that the groom's family pays to his future in-laws before the traditional wedding is celebrated by both families. The dowry consists of money, gifts, and animals (goats, cows, pigs, etc.).

Elephant dance: The elephant dance or "Ndzouh," in the Ndanda-Batoufam language, is probably the most prestigious dance in Bamiléké country. Only the king, the mabatngoup, and the most important notables perform it.

Hijab: This head covering is often worn by Muslim women, though it isn't obligatory in Cameroon. Young girls as well as married women can wear it. It covers hair and arms.

Kapok tree: The kapok tree grows in Mexico, South America, Asia, and Africa. It has many uses. The oil extracted from its seeds is used to make cakes and soaps, and the flowers are used to make perfume. Its leaves, flowers, and young fruit are eaten cooked. Its fibers are used to stuff pillows and mattresses.

Liana: Liana is a type of woody vine or fiber derived from raffia bamboo. It is used to make chairs, roofs, baskets, etc.

Living hedge: The living hedge consists of a row of fresh pickets (sharpened posts) planted in the ground. Though these posts are cut wood, they are able to continue growing, and they form a hedge that is pruned every year.

Mabatngoup: Mabatngoup means "the queen who wears the pelt of the royal panther on her back." Among the Bamilékés, the king is called "the panther" because this animal is the symbol of royalty. Panther pelts and teeth are the property of the king. It's a rare honor to possess them. Only the king, the mabatngoup, and authorized notables have this privilege.

Maka 1 and Maka 2: Sometimes neighborhoods or villages have numbered names. This is done to make it easier to manage larger neighborhoods. When the inhabitants of a village move to create another village, they sometimes give it the name of their former village, adding a number to distinguish them.

Makala: This is the local name for a type of doughnut made with wheat flour, water, sugar, and yeast. The dough is fried in red palm oil, so these are also called palm-oil or red-oil doughnuts.

Ndindim: The ndindim is a plant around 2 meters (6.6 feet) tall, with a large stem at the top and large leaves on either side. It is native to Cameroon and grows in humid environments. Its fruit contains small seeds called peace seeds. These seeds have a slightly minty fragrance and a sweet taste.

The Bamilékés use ndindim to ward off evil spirits, bring good luck and protect themselves. It's common to carry it with you at all times, and to give it as a gift to twins. It can also be used in cooking.

Ndop cloth: Ndop cloth is reserved for kings and nobles. Ordinary people can wear it after accomplishing specific rites or during mourning ceremonies for a relative. All the symbols on ndop cloth have a meaning. For example, the dots represent the panther, a royal animal.

Peanut toffees: Toffees are made with whole peanut seeds, water and sugar, which are boiled to a paste. This paste is then left to cool and harden before being cut into pieces.

Petrol: Gasoline.

Raffia bamboo: Farinifera raffia is a species of palm that thrives in the swamps of western Cameroon. It is also planted in savannahs. It is a great source of wealth for the Bamilékés, given the many products that can be made from it. In particular, it produces a delicious wine—raffia wine.

Sanouh: A word used to greet each other. It is also used to say goodbye.

Shea butter: Shea butter is an edible vegetable oil extracted from the fruit of the shea tree. Shea butter is mainly used for skin and hair care.

Sorrel juice: This is a juice made with red sorrel flowers, water, and sugar. It is drunk chilled.

Text © 2019 Alain Serge Dzotap
Illustrations © 2019 Marc Daniau
Originally published as *Adi de Boutanga* in France
© 2019 Albin Michel
English-language translation © 2025 Alain Serge Dzotap

First published in the United States in 2025
by Eerdmans Books for Young Readers,
an imprint of Wm. B. Eerdmans Publishing Co.
Grand Rapids, Michigan

www.eerdmans.com/youngreaders

All rights reserved

Manufactured in China

33 32 31 30 29 28 27 26 25   1 2 3 4 5 6 7 8 9

ISBN 978-0-8028-5629-6

A catalog record of this book is available from the Library of Congress

Illustrations created with oil on paper

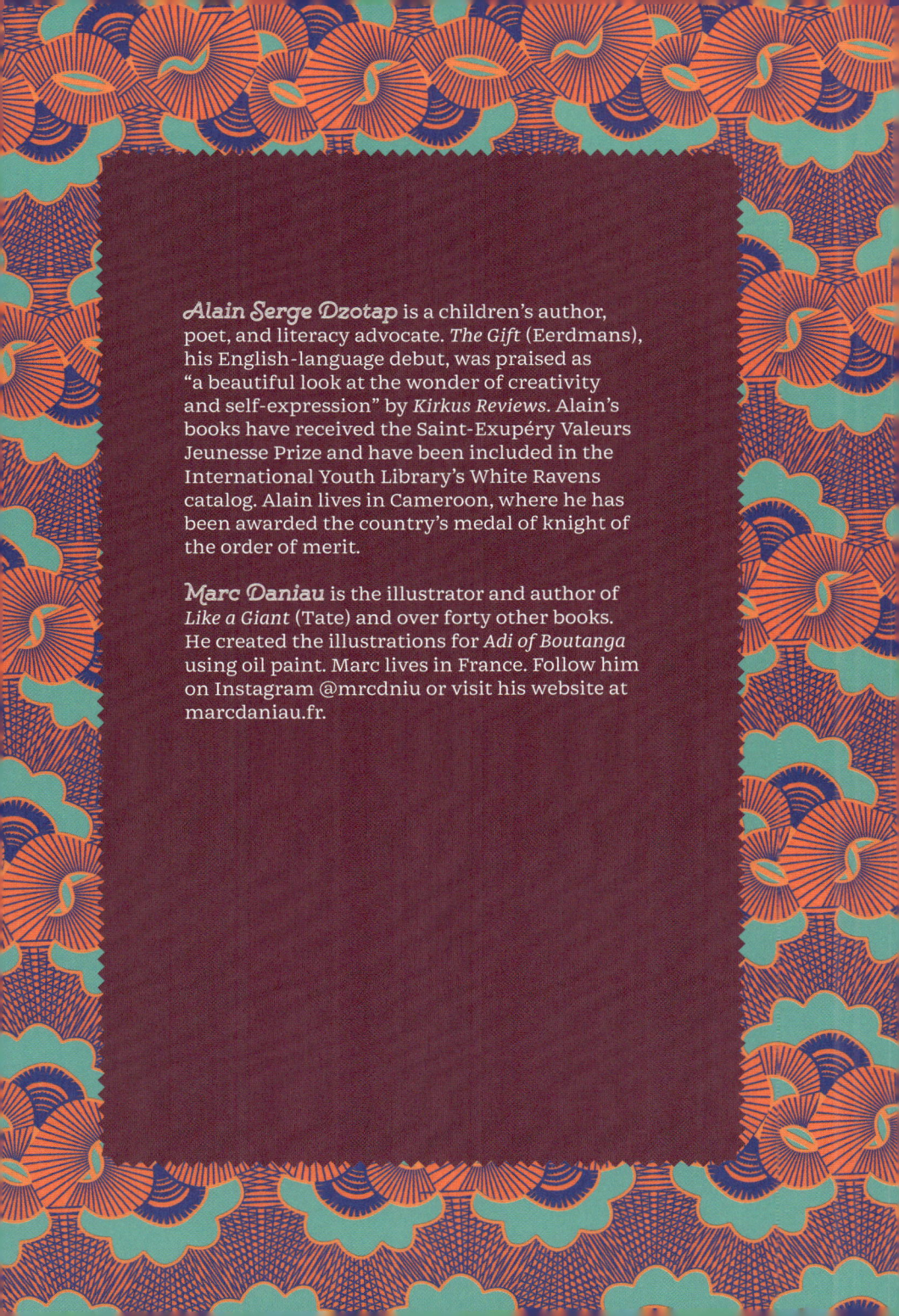

Alain Serge Dzotap is a children's author, poet, and literacy advocate. *The Gift* (Eerdmans), his English-language debut, was praised as "a beautiful look at the wonder of creativity and self-expression" by *Kirkus Reviews*. Alain's books have received the Saint-Exupéry Valeurs Jeunesse Prize and have been included in the International Youth Library's White Ravens catalog. Alain lives in Cameroon, where he has been awarded the country's medal of knight of the order of merit.

Marc Daniau is the illustrator and author of *Like a Giant* (Tate) and over forty other books. He created the illustrations for *Adi of Boutanga* using oil paint. Marc lives in France. Follow him on Instagram @mrcdniu or visit his website at marcdaniau.fr.

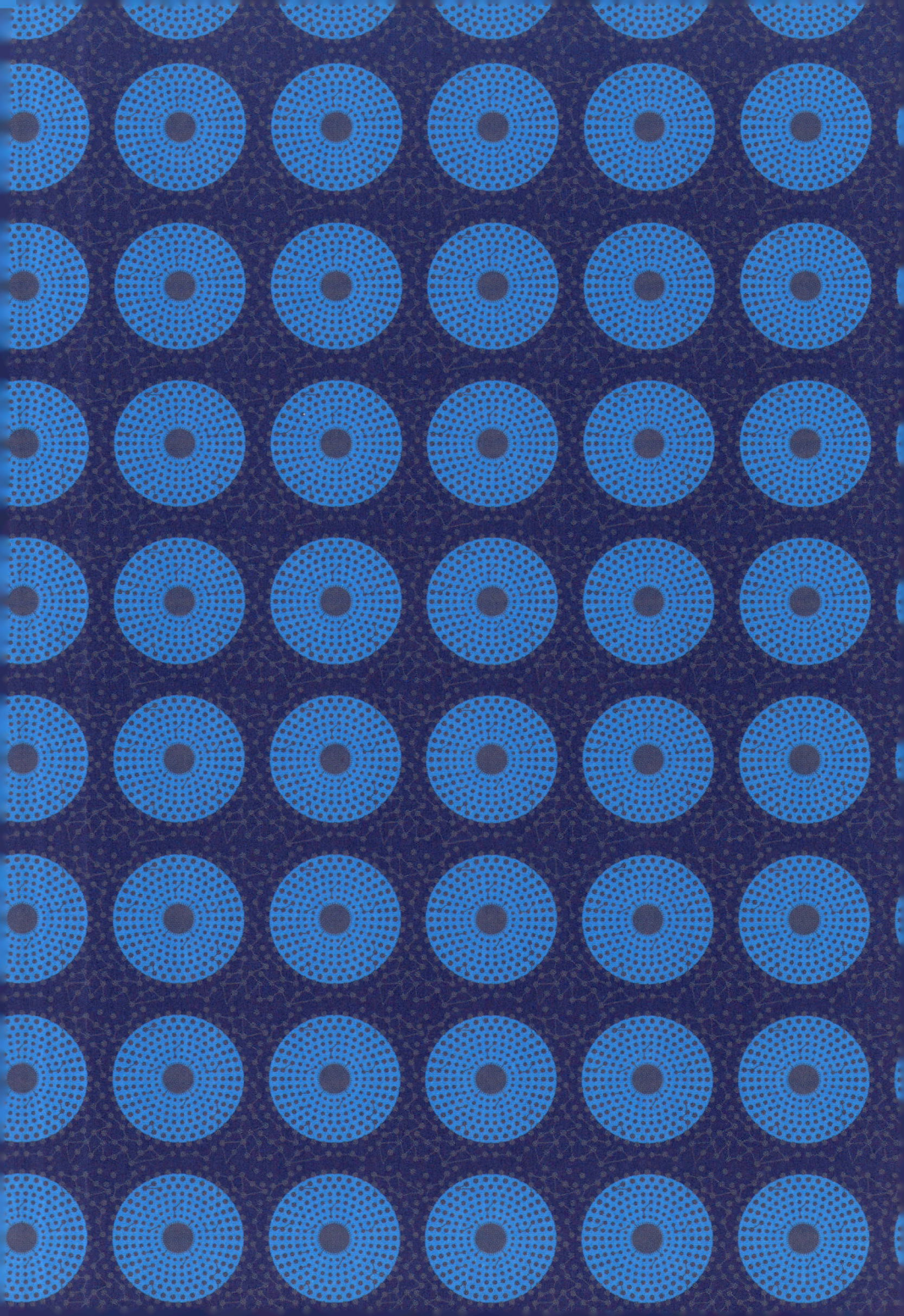